The BACKYARDIGANS

The Secret of Snow

adapted by Alison Inches
based on the original teleplay by Jonny Belt and Robert Scull
illustrated by Dave Aikins

SIMON AND SCHUSTER/NICKELODEON

Based on the TV series *Nick Jr. The Backyardigans*™ as seen on Nick Jr.

SIMON AND SCHUSTER
First published in Great Britain in 2007 by Simon & Schuster UK Ltd
Africa House, 64-78 Kingsway, London WC2B 6AH

Originally published in the USA in 2006 by Simon Spotlight,
an imprint of Simon & Schuster Children's Division, New York.

A CIP catalogue record for this book is available from the British Library

ISBN-10: 1-84738-032-8
ISBN-13: 978-1-84738-032-6

Printed in China

10 9 8 7 6 5 4 3 2 1

Visit our websites www.simonsays.co.uk
                    www.nickjr.co.uk

Once upon a time there was a little girl who loved snow very much. "I love to sledge!" she cried. "I love to catch snowflakes on my tongue! And I love to make snow angels!"

The only problem was that it wasn't snowing. So the little girl decided to try to discover the secret of snow by finding the Ice Lady, who lived far away in the Icy North. Surely the Ice Lady could make it snow!

The little girl set off for the Icy North – a cold, unfriendly place with gloomy, grey skies as far as the eye could see.

The Ice Lady and her assistant were hard at work making the world as icy as possible. The Ice Lady took her job very seriously. She had no time for rest or play, so when she spotted the little girl at her door, she became angry.

"No time for visitors!" she shouted. "To make the world nice, we need to fill it up with ice!"

Then the Ice Lady cranked a wheel on her control panel and sent the little girl swirling in a cyclone of ice cubes all the way . . .

. . . into the middle of a dry, sandy desert.

"Whew!" said the little girl. "How did I get here?"

"Howdy, ma'am!" shouted a passing cowboy. "I'm Cowboy Pablo, and we need to get out of the way of that yonder twister!"

A tornado roared straight towards the little girl and Cowboy Pablo.
It chased them to the left and to the right – and then cornered them
against a rock wall!

"Well, ma'am," said Cowboy Pablo, "it looks like we're goners."

The Ice Lady's assistant, who had been watching the little girl and
Cowboy Pablo from the Ice Factory, could see they needed help.
"I'll freeze the twister with the ice machine!" he cried.
He pushed a button on the control panel, and the twister froze solid.

"Tarnation!" cried Cowboy Pablo. "Is that snow?"

"No," said the little girl. "It's ice. Snow is lighter and fluffier and fun to play in."

Pablo liked the sound of snow, so the two new friends headed north to find the Ice Lady and the secret of snow.

When the Ice Lady saw them coming, she grew annoyed again.
"Oh, for the love of ice!" she cried. "We don't need friendly visitors!
We have *work* to do!"

Again she cranked a wheel on her control panel, and in a swirl of ice
cubes she sent the little girl and Cowboy Pablo tumbling all the way . . .

. . . into a hot, steamy jungle. They landed on the vine of Tyrone of the Jungle. The vine dangled over a deep gorge.

"Gee," said Tyrone of the Jungle, "I wish I could rescue you, but this vine is about to break."

As the rope gave way, the Ice Lady's assistant, who had been watching everything, turned the waterfall into an icy slide. The friends slid to safety.

Then the little girl told her new friend all about her journey. Tyrone of the Jungle loved the sound of snow, so he joined the others on their trip back to the Icy North.

When the friends returned to the Ice Factory, the Ice Lady became angrier than ever. She switched on her ice machine and froze everything inside her factory. The children – and the Ice Lady's assistant – tried to escape, but they slipped on the ice and slid onto the factory floor.

"No more interruptions!" boomed the Ice Lady. "Now you will make ice for me! Get to work!"

But the friends found they liked to make ice – and this did not please the Ice Lady one bit. Ice making was serious business. The angrier she got, the faster she cranked her ice machine. It went berserk, and her office filled up with ice.

"Help!" she screamed.

The Ice Lady's workers rushed to her office and pulled her out of the ice.
"You saved me!" said the Ice Lady with great surprise.
"Of course we did!" said the Ice Lady's assistant.
"That's what friends are for!" said the little girl.

"We didn't mean to interrupt your work," the little girl went on. "We just wanted to find out the secret of snow."

"I'm sorry," said the Ice Lady, who looked quite humbled. "But I don't know the secret of snow."

The little girl felt awful. Now it wasn't going to snow, and she had let down her friends. On top of that, she had disrupted the Ice Lady. "I'm so sorry," said the little girl glumly.

"When you've got good friends," said the Ice Lady, "who cares about snow?"

And just then, as if by magic, it began to snow.

And so Tyrone of the Jungle and Cowboy Pablo got their wish to see snow for the first time. And the little girl got to play in the backyard with all of her friends!